M.P. 1   University.
Since 1988 h   children's books.
Amor   an Patten,
The Bed   *melly History*
with Mary   th Robert Bolt.
His previou   *ch the Moon* and
Ice Tra   th Hooper.
M. P. Robertso   or Sophy Williams,

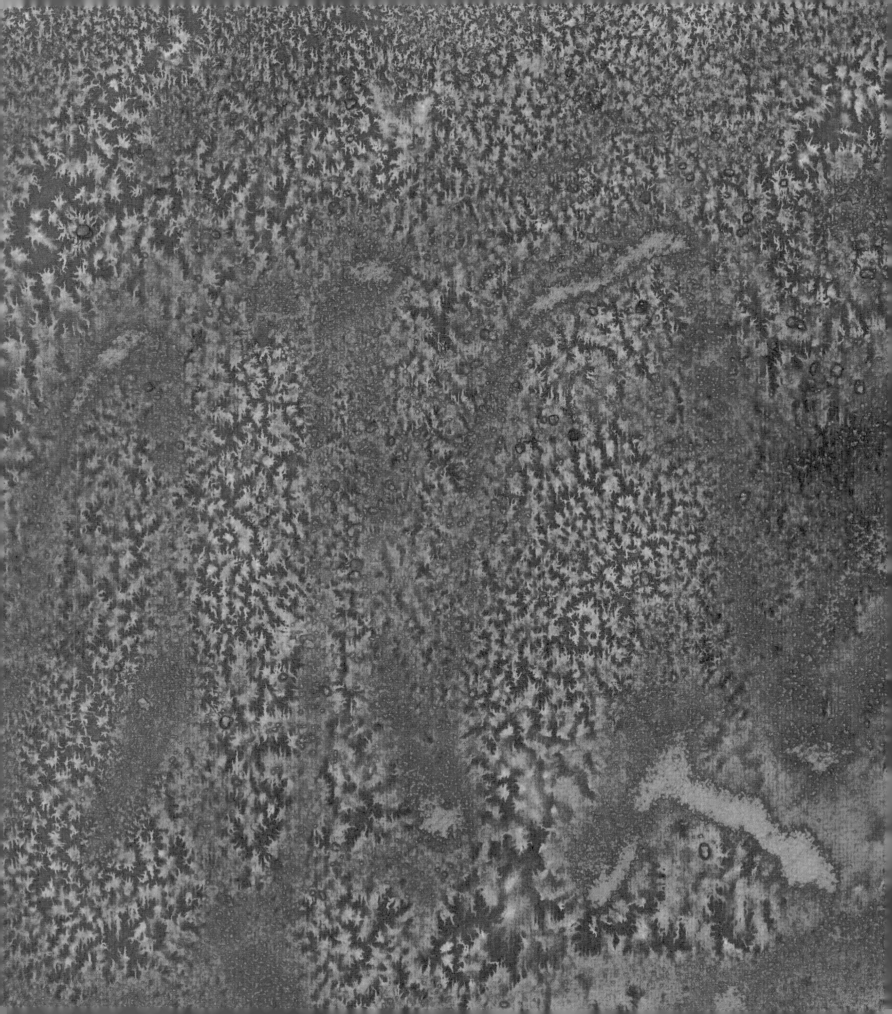

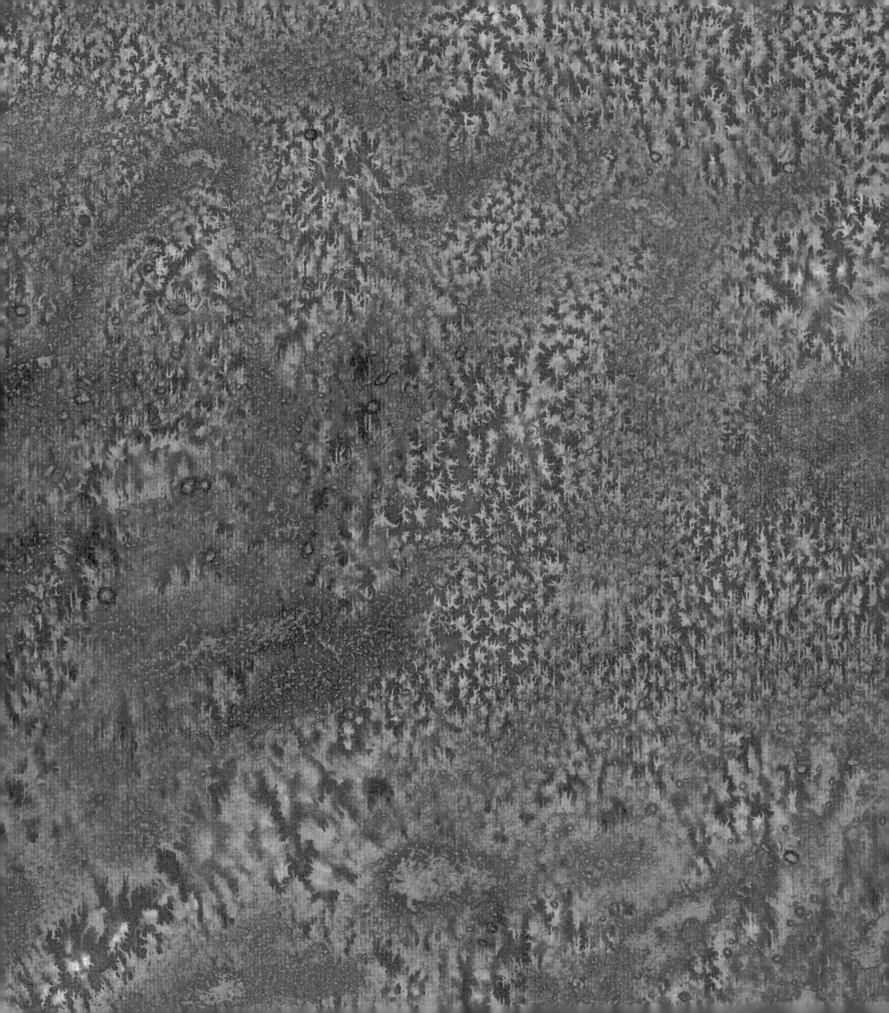

For Osky Bosky Boy (Oscar) – *M.P.R.*

The Egg copyright © Frances Lincoln Limited 2000
Text and illustrations copyright © M.P. Robertson 2000

First published in Great Britain in 2000 by
Frances Lincoln Limited, 4 Torriano Mews,
Torriano Avenue, London NW5 2RZ

British Library Cataloguing in Publication Data available on request

ISBN 0-7112-1524-3 hardback
ISBN 0-7112-1525-1 paperback

Printed in Hong Kong

1 3 5 7 9 8 6 4 2

The
EGG

M.P. Robertson

FRANCES LINCOLN

G eorge knew something wasn't
right, when he found more than
he had bargained for under his mother's
favourite chicken.

He moved the egg to the warmth
of his bedroom. For three days
and three nights he read the egg stories.

On the third night, the egg started to rumble.

Something was hatching, and it definitely wasn't a chicken …

When the dragon saw George, it gave a chirrup of delight.

George didn't speak Dragon, but he knew exactly what the dragon had said ...
"Mummy."

George had never been a mother before, but he knew that it was his motherly duty to teach the dragon dragony ways.

 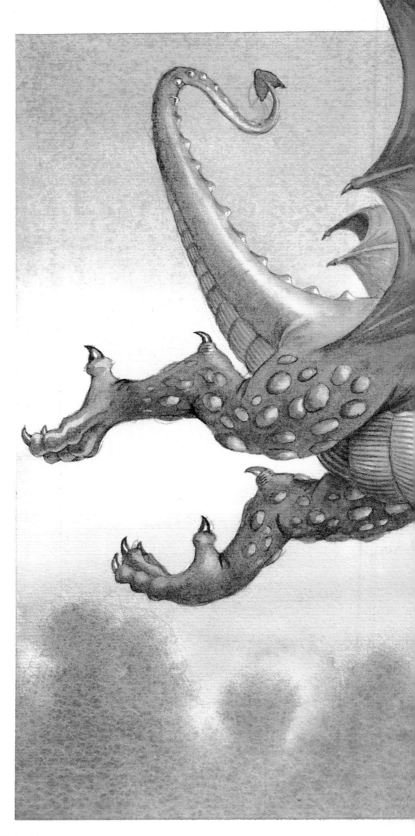

The first lesson he taught was *The Fine Art of Flying.*

The second lesson was *Fire and How to Breathe It.*

The third lesson was *How to Distress a Damsel*.

And the final lesson was *How to Duff a Knight*.

Every evening, as all good mothers should, George read the dragon a bedtime story.

One night, as he read from a book of dragon tales, the dragon looked longingly at the pictures. A sizzling tear rolled down his scaly cheek.

The dragon was lonely. He was missing his own kind.

The next morning, the dragon had gone.
George was very sad. He thought he
would never see his dragon again.

But seven nights later, he was woken
by the beating of wings. Excitedly, he
pulled back the curtains. There, perched in
the tree, was the dragon. George opened
the window and clambered onto his back.

They soared into the night, chasing the moon around the world, over oceans and mountains and cities.

Faster and faster they went, until they came to a place that was neither North nor South, East nor West.

They swooped down through
the clouds, into a cave that gaped
like a dragon's jaws. This was the
place where dragons lived.
    The dragon gave a roar
of delight. He was home at last.

Finally, it was time for George to leave.
  Up, up they flew, chasing sleep through the night,
until they could see his home below.

George hugged his dragon tight,
and the dragon gave a roar. George
didn't speak Dragon, but he knew
exactly what the dragon had said …

… "Thank you."

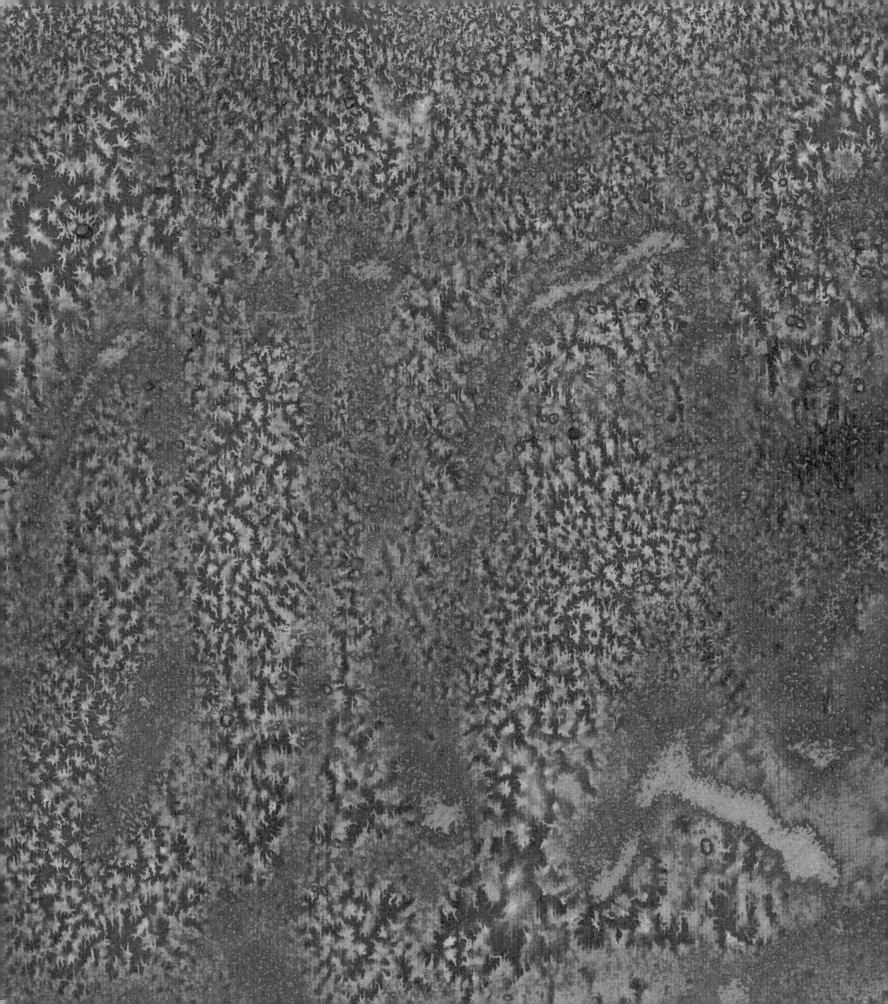

MORE PICTURE BOOKS IN PAPERBACK
FROM FRANCES LINCOLN

SEVEN WAYS TO CATCH THE MOON
Mark Robertson

There are seven ways to catch the moon… Follow a little girl's dream
as she tried hitching with a witch, riding on a dragon's back
and floating in a hot-air balloon, in this beautifully illustrated fantasy.

Suitable for Early Years Education and for National Curriculum English – Reading, Key Stage 1
Scottish Guidelines English Language – Reading, Level A

ISBN 0-7112-1413-1 £5.99

MISSING!
Jonathan Langley

It's the first day of the holidays, but no one has told Daisy's cat Lupin.
So he's at the corner as usual waiting for Daisy to come home,
while she's inside… looking for him!

Suitable for Nursery Education and for National Curriculum English – Reading, Key Stage 1
Scottish Guidelines English Language – Reading, Level A

ISBN 0-7112-1543-X £5.99

ELLIE'S GROWL
Karen Popham

Ellie loves it when her brother reads her books about animals, because he
makes wonderful animal noises. One day, Ellie learns that she, too can growl
like a tiger – with some quite unexpected results!

Suitable for Nursery Education and for National Curriculum English – Reading, Key Stage 1
Scottish Guidelines English Language – Reading, Levels A and B

ISBN 0-7112-1505-7 £5.99

Frances Lincoln titles are available from all good bookshops.
Prices are correct at time of publication, but may be subject to change.

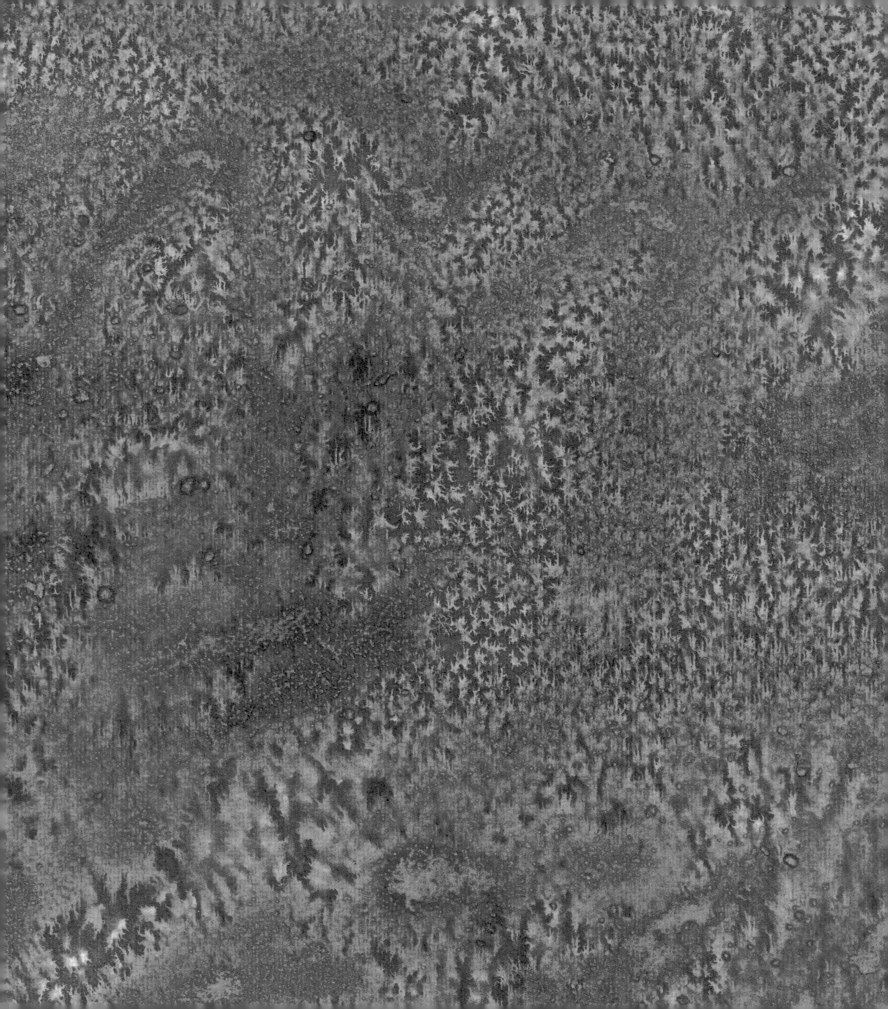